Even Bread Has a Home

Contents

Written by Zac Sutton

Illustrated by Martin Bailey

Families Are Important

Tomas and Amaryllis were tortillas and they were best friends.

One day, as they were looking in the window of a bakery, Tomas said to Amaryllis, "Have you ever wondered where tortillas come from? Have you ever thought that there might be hundreds of tortillas somewhere? Not just a few like there are here?"

"Yes, I have," replied Amaryllis. "It'd be wonderful if we could find out where we came from. Look at all those breads in there. I wonder if any of them can tell us?"

"There's a raisin loaf. Let's ask her," Amaryllis said.

The raisin loaf had a sticky shiny top and raisins poking out of her round sides, but she looked friendly enough.

"Excuse me, Raisin Loaf, do you know how we could find our families?" Tomas asked politely. "Do you know where tortillas come from?"

"I'm sorry, but I've never been out of the country," replied the raisin loaf. "My family has always lived in England. There are many different breads here, but I've never seen a lot of tortillas. So I don't think your family comes from here. The best way for you to find out where you came from is to travel. You could ask wherever you smell freshly-baked bread."

Tomas and Amaryllis thanked the raisin loaf. "Good luck," she said, winking one of her raisins at them. "It may take a while, but I'm sure in the end you'll find where you come from."

The Start of the Search – French Bread

Amaryllis and Tomas decided to start their search right away. They hurried to the airport and hid themselves away in the galley of a plane.

"I'm scared," said Amaryllis, as the plane took off. "This is a big adventure."

"Don't worry, Amaryllis," Tomas said. "I feel a bit scared too, but won't it be great to find our families and to know where we came from and where our roots are?"

Soon the plane landed in Paris, France. The cabin crew wheeled the food carts to the terminal, with Tomas and Amaryllis hiding inside. Quickly, the tortillas jumped out and made their way to a nearby bakery.

In the window, and inside the bakery, were rows and rows of baguettes, long skinny French sticks, and croissants, but there were no tortillas.

"Too bad," said Tomas sadly. "Our families certainly aren't here. Let's go back to the airport and get on another plane."

So Tomas and Amaryllis crept back out of the door of the bakery and went down the busy street to the airport.

"Let's get on this plane," said Amaryllis. "It looks as if it's leaving soon."

Once again, the galley seemed the best place to hide. So Tomas and Amaryllis hid under the lid of a big silver serving dish, beside a long garlic bread.

'You know, we don't even know where this plane is going," sighed Amaryllis. "We could end up anywhere."

"Maybe the garlic bread can tell us," said Tomas.

But when they peeped out, the garlic bread was gone.

The Danish Sourdough Loaf

When the plane landed, the little tortillas hid in the cart like they had before.

"I'm freezing," whispered Amaryllis, as they were being wheeled to the terminal. "Let's see if we can find the smell of warm baking bread. Hopefully this will be home."

The airport terminal was very big. "Sniff," said Tomas, "and when we smell baking bread, we'll jump off the cart."

"Now, come on, follow me," said Amaryllis, as she jumped off the cart and ran over to where the smell of baking bread was coming from.

"Here they are," said Tomas. "Look at the rows of loaves."

"You look and smell amazing," Amaryllis said to a big loaf. "But do you have any tortillas here? We're looking for our families."

"No, not here," said the large crusty loaf.

"What country are we in now?" asked Tomas.

"You're in Denmark," said the crusty loaf. "I'm Danish Sourdough. I'm afraid you won't find your families here. The Roti family lives nearby, though. They may be able to help you."

The Rotis

Danish Sourdough told Tomas and Amaryllis how to find the Indian family. Nervously, they knocked on the door.

It was opened by a very thin, very tall, golden brown roti. Beside him, little rotis pushed and shoved each other, trying to see the visitors.

"Hello," said Tomas shyly. "I'm Tomas Tortilla and this is my friend Amaryllis. We're trying to find our families."

"Danish Sourdough thought you might be able to help us," said Amaryllis.

"Come inside," said Father Roti with a welcoming smile. "We have guests," he called to Mother Roti.

The smell of spices floated through the house as Mother Roti came through the kitchen door. She was the same beautiful golden brown as Father Roti, but not as tall.

She opened her arms wide. "Welcome to our home," she said. "How can we help you?"

So, while the little Rotis rolled and tumbled over them, Tomas and Amaryllis told Father and Mother Roti about their adventures so far and how they were searching for their families.

When they finished their story, Father Roti said, "I think you come from Mexico. We'll look in the atlas. That will show us Mexico. I've heard that there are tortilla families there. In fact, I think that is where they all come from."

"There it is!" exclaimed Father Roti, looking through the atlas. "Just below California in the United States."

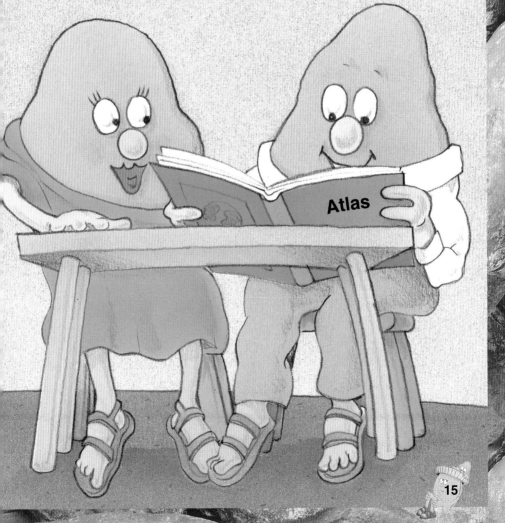

The Flight Plan

"But how will we get to Mexico from Denmark?" asked Tomas.

"I'll call the travel agency for you," replied Mother Roti. "They'll tell us how to get you to Mexico."

The travel agent told Mother Roti that to get to Mexico, they must first fly to Frankfurt, in Germany. Then they would fly to Los Angeles, California, and then on to Tijuana, Mexico.

"I'll make some reservations," said Father Roti gently. "You can't just keep getting on planes."

That night Tomas and Amaryllis stayed with the Roti family. Father Roti told them how it was that he and Mother Roti had come to live in Denmark.

'We always liked adventure," he said. "When we were young we visited many countries. When we got here we liked it. So we stayed."

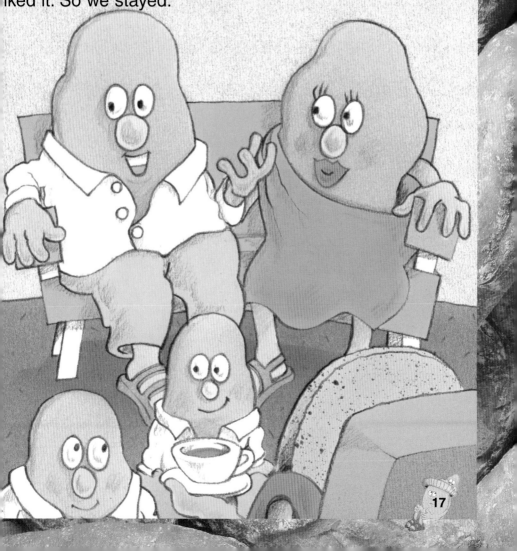

"Many breads are like us," he continued. "They travel so much. Even though a country may have its own special bread, you can find different breads all over the world."

"Take our cousins, the Naan family," said Mother Roti. "You can find them in lots of countries these days. Some people even mistake us for Naans because they can look like us."

"Germany is the home of pumpernickel and black breads," said Father Roti. "They are dark and have a lot of seeds in them."

"Your next stop is Frankfurt," said Mother Roti. "You should meet some pumpernickels there."

Frau Pumpernickel Loaf and Friends

Soon it was time for Tomas and Amaryllis to go to the airport. The Roti family went to see them off.

"Good luck!" Mother Roti called. "When you find your families, please write and give us your address."

Tomas and Amaryllis waved sadly.

"Thank you for being so kind to us," they called. "We'll keep in touch."

The flight to Frankfurt was soon over.

"Remember what Mother Roti said. We must find the German breads," said Tomas.

"I smell bread," said Amaryllis, as she ran around the corner with Tomas following.

Crash! They collided with an airport security guard.

"Look where you're going!" the guard said as he looked at them strangely. "Goodness me! I've never seen anything like you before. Who are you? What are you? Where are you going?"

Tomas said, "We are tortillas and we're on our way to Mexico to find our families. But right now we'd like to meet some German breads."

The security guard said, "Oh, that's no trouble. I'll take you to meet some German breads."

He picked Tomas and Amaryllis up and popped them in a basket. Then he walked along quickly, swinging the basket from side to side. The little breads laughed. It was like being on a roller coaster ride.

"I can see the breads!" shouted Amaryllis, as they arrived at a bakery. "This is fun."

There were rows and rows of breads in the bakery. There were plump stollen, pumpernickel loaves, and black breads. The guard put the basket on the shelf beside the German breads. Tomas and Amaryllis peeped out shyly.

23

"Guten Morgen," said an enormous pumpernickel loaf with a heavy German accent, "I'm pleased to meet you."

She sounded as if she was speaking through molasses.

"Good morning, ma'am," Tomas and Amaryllis replied.

"Allow me to present Gerda Stollen and Berta Black Bread," the security guard said.

The two loaves smiled and said, "You are most unusual looking. We've only known round breads – more solid breads. You are very thin."

"I guess our whole family is thin," Amaryllis said, feeling a bit upset.

"Don't be upset," said Frau Pumpernickel Loaf. "We're all special in our own way. We're all loved for being just as we are."

"Time to go," said the airport security guard. "Your flight's boarding. I'll take you to the plane."

Being Famous

It seemed like only seconds and the plane was landing in Los Angeles.

In the terminal, Tomas sniffed the air again. "Just look at all those burger buns," he said.

"Welcome to America!" said a soft burger bun. "My name is Hank Hamburger. You must be Tomas and Amaryllis!"

"How did you know our names?" asked Tomas.

"You're famous!" replied Hank. "You've been in all the newspapers. Everyone knows you're looking for your roots. Everyone knows you're trying to find where your families came from."

Tomas and Amaryllis were amazed. They had never dreamed they would be famous.

Many breads came up to meet them. There were pretzels, bagels, American sourdoughs, a lot of hamburger buns, and even matzo breads from Israel. They all wanted to talk to the famous little tortillas.

They all talked and talked about their lives, where they lived now, and where they wanted to travel to. They were still talking when the flight to Mexico was called.

"Good luck," called the breads as Tomas and Amaryllis boarded the plane.

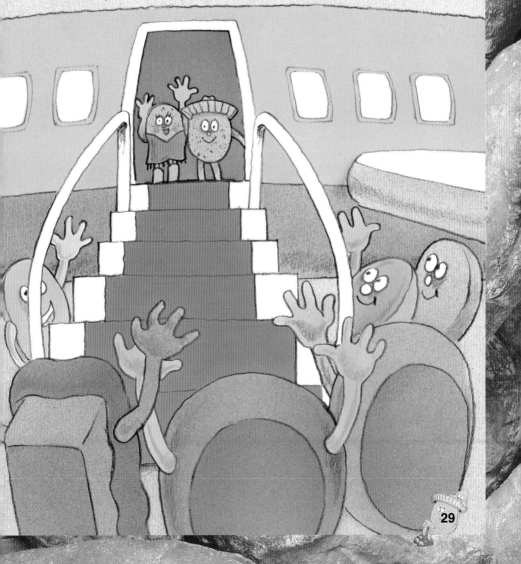

Home at Last

Tomas and Amaryllis were so excited that they couldn't sit still on the plane. At last they landed in Tijuana. The airport was crowded. Everywhere they looked, they saw breads. There were rows and rows of golden breads, breads of every shape and size. But best of all, breads that looked exactly like Tomas and Amaryllis.

And right in the front was the Tortilla family. They carried a big banner which said:

Welcome home, Tomas and Amaryllis!
We're proud of you and we love you!

As Tomas and Amaryllis came down the steps, they were hugged and kissed. They were lifted high and carried to a limousine. They were driven through the city and given a ticker-tape parade.

At last they had found where they belonged and where their families were from. They had also learned that all kinds of breads are welcome all over the world.

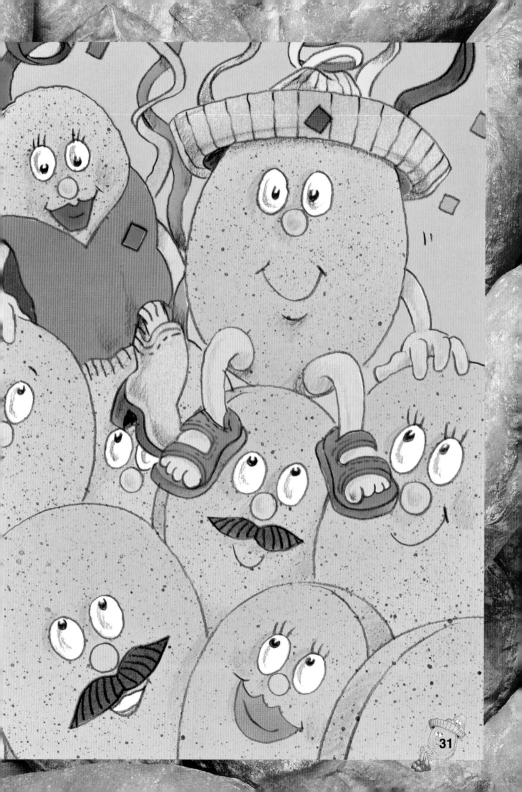

As they drove into the Mexican countryside, they could see the fields of corn stretching away into the distance.

This was where it had all started for their families.